STARLIGHT IN TWO MILLION

STARLIGHT IN TWO MILLION

A Neo-Scientific Novella

$$\infty - 0 - a * g + 0 = \infty$$

AMY CATANZANO

NOEMI PRESS

LIBRARY OF CONGRESS CATALOGUING-IN-PUBLICATION DATA
Catanzano, Amy.
Starlight in Two Million / Amy Catanzano.
ISBN 978-1-934819-39-5 (pbk.)
LIBRARY OF CONGRESS CONTROL NUMBER: 2014930556

Cover art by Vance Kirkland (1904-81), *Four Suns in Space* (1971), oil on linen, 75" x 139," courtesy of Kirkland Museum of Fine & Decorative Art, Denver

Cover design by Evan Lavender-Smith
Interior design by Amy Catanzano
Typeset in Minion, Galliard, Eurostile, Futura, and Wilson Greek

Distributed to the trade by Small Press Distribution
www.spdbooks.org

Published by Noemi Press
Mesilla Park, New Mexico
www.noemipress.org

CONTENTS

Stella writes the library. From the library in her ship to the one in space, she makes the distance. She knows that reading is writing, in one sense, but also knows there is nothing like actual writing to cultivate an awareness of the materiality of everything, of text as fuel.

LAURA MORIARTY
Ultravioleta

Is there a 4th person narration?

SHANXING WANG
Mad Science in Imperial City

The Greeks called the unconcealedness of beings *aletheia*. We say "truth" and think little enough in using this word.

MARTIN HEIDEGGER
Poetry, Language, Thought

The soul is wheedled by Love who looks exactly like an iridescent veil and assumes the masked face of a chrysalis. It walks upon inverted skulls. Behind the wall where it hides, claws brandish weapons. It is baptized with poison. Ancient monsters, the wall's substance, laugh into their green beards. The heart remains red and blue, violet in the artificial absence of the iridescent veil that it is weaving.

ALFRED JARRY
*Exploits & Opinions of Doctor Faustroll, Pataphysician:
A Neo-Scientific Novel*

WMAP

Like everyone offworld, I used my time in the gallery of maps to further an agenda. It was this feeling of empire I chose to collide. As if buried inside the shore you make capillary shapes to. Because if the world is anthropic. We could spend our entire lives plucking the interplanetary pearls from our hearts.

You are just like the others, she notes. Surveying continents, their lavish names.

Continents have wings, I confess. From above, all labyrinths look alike.

Solar systems, as bound objects, are never fully available to my needs. In astronomy—that black drapery of the stars—revolution is a return to a starting point. Deep in the curve of my heart, as if the sea weren't underneath. I do the math for fresh water. Spirals are for pleasure. Above, in the cult of what would happen if we had choices, would we know it?

A particle physicist by profession, she was schooled in both charm and beauty states. I develop theories that apply at all distance scales. This is no gift but rather a candlelight spell for prosperity. Leakages are common and do not dissuade me. Pranks happen frequently. It's the one stipulation behind the cloak.

She brings the lamp closer. What is the definition between love, she asks, and its future?

One circumnavigates the body, looking for a generator, a wayward skin. Mine is part myth, half demolished, fully waking.

Yours moves in waves, she says, so that when we combine, we are extraordinary.

This is the future, I respond. Love is the hybrid of us all.

I want to live like that, she claims. In particular, when you exist, you live like the trees, bifurcated, and then like the storms, uncertain.

The rebel strikes, I mouth. From the discordian shore, ripple the edge in my direction. Let that vantage fever. Undo its root.

She hesitates. Non-locality aside, much of the difficulty is in the assumptions, she says. It always is.

Like a pyramid appearing over our greatest city, I propose. Can you imagine it? The air quiet with lightning. Galaxies unwinding the word from the book.

A poem is a pilot, she writes. And satellites and species.

A poem is high-frequency, we read. On first contact we glide to the hum of an invisible engine.

You're a rocketship, I radio.

We spacewalk, she says.

Like sex—the kind that pushes the hottest weather patterns out to the front, to be seen. Since skin buckles and rains. Through its lines, I type, in superstrings, in streaks.

It is in this sense that all language, I remember.

Unconcealed, she prompts.

We devolve in certain waters. I head away from ethernity and begin to speak as it speaks me.

The Becoming of Memory

How does anything shimmer beyond its borders? I found courage in the parody of my theory of the machine. That's how singularities end, Aletheia thinks. Speculatively. As long as I hold on to it, you will write me. I will be borderless for you, and you, in return, will border me.

Once across she performs the experiment from the inside out. Hours in, she hears a voice behind her.

Words prevent fading more than they reveal, the voice states.

Aletheia turns around. Something emerges from the largest of her test tubes.

Unlike Aletheia, the visitor did not need a name. Its gravity was strong. It resisted the idea of its final form, and this pleased it. But the visitor was dangerous. Whereas Aletheia was narrow, the visitor was one of many, a ghost from the inner colonies. As when implicating something, it would ask, what divides the world from the war? Using the land we know.

It's been too long, Aletheia says.

I thought we weren't concerned with time anymore, the visitor grins.

You got me there, Aletheia says.

The visitor remarks on her predicament.

That's why I need to find Epoché, Aletheia explains.

The visitor nods. I'm headed to the temporary autonomous zones. I imagine you haven't been there, to the surveillance ruins? Can I bring you back anything? the visitor laughs.

Aletheia relaxes. I've heard about the temporary autonomous zones, she says. Like you, they are something of a legend.

They are entryways, the visitor admits.

The government's physics, Aletheia whispers.

Aletheia knew inside the farthest planet in her mind that a forest was always clearing. The surveillance ruins were no place for her. She needed to find Epoché. So they would join forces against the war. If they hadn't already. This would require an extropian's perspective.

And everything that is detected, like art, the visitor interrupts, assembling space so that she can read between the lines.

We will split the unsuspecting flatlanders right in half! Aletheia declares, then shifts her gaze to the crowns of semperviviams nesting the doorway. Nearby, the quilled chrysanthemums bloom spherically, sprayed, and thread-petaled. Even out of focus, I prefer the cornflower or blue bottle, just like the beloved music from an instrument you once knew and played.

The World Worlds

Epoché knows that his best chance to steal the *iEpiphany* will be when the authorities focus their efforts on the planet's surface, where festival activities will be most prominent.

In earlier times, there were dozens of festivals per year, each one marking a solar month. But that was when the planet orbited its sun much faster. As the planet's orbit slowed while the multiverse accelerated, biological and geological changes occurred. One of the most pronounced changes on this slowing world was the practice of extreme classification, a result of the perceived increase in complexity. Taxonomy grew into the world's most significant economical force.

Adapting had not been easy. Epoché spent most of his time in the information halls hoping to find a way to dismantle the text from lock down. How would he gain access to the *iEpiphany*'s holding cell?

Under the Ocean Floor

Dear Epoché, Aletheia writes.

Like a timescale, I am locating you. Begin recording. At the center of my galaxy swirls a supermassive black hole, formed from a dying star. *Gravity always wins*, the stars flare. Black holes are a site where information disappears from perception, never to be redistributed in any detectable form. An endpoint of spacetime, the black hole swirling in the center of my galaxy was once a burning sun. End recording. This is an allegory of space and time and how each word became one.

My heart, Aletheia

Bright Line Spectrum

Many years ago, if the average individual read the *iEpiphany* at all, they did so out of simple curiosity. The title evokes a Romantic agency, albeit one multiplied by technological prosthetics.

The *iEpiphany* behaves like a hypothetical canvas that is only finished when framed. It would be idle to deny that it is a calculated book. Why, in many quarters, its reputation went into eclipse must be explained. The *iEpiphany* was once considered to be *All Exteriors*. Others made it *A Sign of Secrets*. Some individuals give it a one-word designation, *Hyperbiography*. Still others added a subtitle: *iEpiphany: Suspending Closure*.

But it is safe to say now the *iEpiphany* has undergone a reversal of fortune. Like other ships of spacetime, it travels. These trips have to do with what is, or what could be, the relationship of the imagination to consciousness, and what are the limits, if any, of language itself.

Predominantly

The city is a circuit. Where do we support life? the billboards blink. And where do we end it?

With the *iEpiphany* finally in hand, Epoché boards the designated vessel to begin making contact with Aletheia. The vessel does not carry its passengers by moving. Instead, it remains stationary while reorganizing the setting around it.

Feeling the slowing world disappear, he thinks about Aletheia, longs for her pirate broadcast. Shapes emerge. A skin of blue water is in the distance. A blur of greenery. Blue hearts loosen themselves from underneath the sea. Like the rings that layer through us. Greenery is loosened from the skin of blue water. Between rings, hearts, there's greenery. Hearts loosen themselves into place.

Epoché reaches into his bag for the thieving device. He's surprised to find the *iEpiphany* so much heavier aboard the vessel. He rubs the small wings colored by the twinkling pinks of a starry nebula. Will Aletheia remember him according to her version of history?

Hunching forward on his seat, he listens to the intermittent crests of the powerful engines that carry him.

Or is that the ocean?

As an epiphenomenon, the war is fought on several fronts, a feedback loop arguing the weapons forward.

But this way of thinking was not new. The masquerading face of the war adapts to every side. No one knows what will result from the translations. Thankfully, Epoché is in contact with several negotiators within the war. But he hasn't been able to convince them that we are approaching the shock waves. Or, rather, that the shock waves are approaching us.

Which represents a new kind of collision in space.

There are exceptions. Unrestricted permissions.

I have lived this gateway a dozen times, Epoché thinks. And the genealogies, those tiny pellets, always part.

The Imaginary Present

Dear Aletheia, Epoché writes.

I hope this finds you submerged in the life you pursue wandering, where the Theory of the Derivé most certainly flourishes, which I also hold in the highest regard. Its warped surface. However, as you must be aware, there is some urgency to my communication, as I would never break cover without extraordinary reasons, but, alas, here I am. Let me be clear: a new translation has been located. And the theater we will inevitably find there. I know I shouldn't convey too much, but I must, please forgive me, communicate what I think are the precise coordinates. I am hoping I will be by your side to investigate. But I am undecided if you will remember me. I still question the role I played in your social morphology and the later role I played in the first navigational charts of the sentient continents. Now, for the center jewel: I have obtained the *iEpiphany*. It will be transmitting shortly.

Helicoidally yours, Epoché

Blueshifts

It begins slowly with a civilization. A blue sail. The picture she makes is an observatory from space. The same degree of curvature at every location, it is a language that is a dwelling.

She uses the colors for their charges. Out of the particular. She gathers and unites the picture. Which acts like a mirror. The picture traces her speech. Which is really the mouth of a voyage and a massive net sifting blue waters. At the end of the world the ship empties its contents. Nothing remains of my castle in the air. Believing as we do, in the explorer you seem to be. Aletheia recites the story she has heard a thousand times. Its astroscience frees her.

Waking, she feels her dreaming body emerge as if being pushed from underground. She stretches. The room gets louder, more prominent. Quickly she uploads. Feels for the patterned lock. The pattern is like a library. The library is like a town. The town is like a drift. The drift is like a cloud. The cloud is like an eye. The eye is like a hook. The hook is like a rare wing. The wing is like her rapid heart, its cellular automata patterning for clues. It used to be difficult, but, with time, she grew stronger, more perceptive.

Aletheia checks the transmission for authenticity. It's brighter than she expected. Denser, like a star.

According to some interpretations, the *iEpiphany* is a treatise for disinformation. But it's something else that secures our place in the war, which we don't quite see, our place. The war appears as though it's in a bubble somewhere floating up and down along rivers, to the side, upside down over mountains that don't look like mountains, over cities that don't look like cities, over families that don't look like families. And the bubble is suspended at times, stops. When we look into the bubble through its transparent film, our vision becomes a curtain. Between the war and myself. And situated inside a different bubble, one that is self-created, like all the others, I believe that no one really dies, no one really dies.

I don't, Aletheia thinks. Except that when I die, I am made into a dwelling that is a language. Aletheia's cities are not cities, her mountains are not mountains, the river running through the foreground is not a river but an artery into her heart.

And the bubble is detectable only by how everything outside of it behaves.

At the beginning of the day when the waves are calm and the water recedes, when the sun lights the beach house in her memory that is her home, the bubble, like all bubbles, dissolves, releasing its ephemera into the blue sea to be sifted by massive nets for signs of treasure.

Fast Forward

Epoché is used to thinking only in the present moment so that when he sees someone leave a room, he thinks that they are no longer experiencing the room. Since everyone operates the present under different circumstances, transitions are especially challenging.

For those born in the present, others enter and leave our immediate experience while we remain. But Epoché has not always been of the present. He has experienced time in the past, even if it was an illusion. His future is sometimes angular. Distributed in folds. An origami releasing in the mind.

Ubiquitously, he considers time through the capsule of his skin.

Soon I will see Aletheia, he thinks. We will sabotage the medium is the message. The very condition of our survival.

Take-off

Dear Epoché, Aletheia writes.

I could see the whole city from the sky. The view was deceptive. All we could see were the trees. Even from the surface of space, the diameter of roads appeared swollen. I remember hearing that some astronauts who have been to space never dream about space, have never once, in all their days since, dreamt about space. As for now, the crops hold steady.

Out of sight, out of mind, Aletheia

Two Acts

Dear Aletheia, Epoché writes.

One by one, fireflies burn as if performing acts of self-worship. The river in late spring seizes its own urgency. Each leaf falls from the favor of its tree. On the hour, leaves gather on the ground, signaling the end of Act I.

Act II begins again, Epoché

Wavelengths

Dear Epoché, Aletheia writes.

I wonder that, too, if every light we see is a star.

Aletheia

How to Construct a Time Machine

Dear Aletheia, Epoché writes.

First, locate the poem's equator. Find the black hole at the center of its galaxy. It might seem to rotate in one direction. Like water on this side of things. We will meet on the other side. Out the back and through the centerline where It is Never Either Or.

Time as seen from the machine,
Epoché

Resurfacing

Dear Epoché, Aletheia writes.

Looking through the opal aurora—

with fever, A

Earth, Redux, Majesty

Dear Aletheia, Epoché writes.

Are spirals also questions?

Epoché

On Morality

Dear Epoché, Aletheia writes.

What is in this moment but a command, imageless, that demands that this moment fills itself with the songs of the other, or empties itself into those who witness the blackbirds emptying the heavy evening into themselves, and we listen

and wonder? Aletheia

Shooting Stars

Windows mirror the wild foliage and fractal shoreline. Epoché wonders how he'll find Aletheia in this unwritten maze. A force field momentarily flickers as he approaches then disappears again as he is granted admittance.

Once inside Aletheia's lab, he notices the sweetness in the air. Flowers must be growing. Windows look out onto the darkening ocean. It is nearly evening. He finds Aletheia sitting in a chair with electrodes hooked to her hands, pressing buttons attached to a device extending from above her. Populating the air in front of her, smoky signs quickly materialize and dissipate.

Seeing Epoché, Aletheia presses a series of buttons to freeze the signs into place. She separates herself from the device and heads over to him. They embrace.

Did you receive my transmission? Epoché asks. Aletheia's hair and clothing swirl. The ocean towers in the background.

Every word, Aletheia confirms.

I wasn't sure if you would remember me, Epoché confesses. The room's diffused light is in contrast to the sharpness of Aletheia's eyes.

Epoché scans the frozen signs hovering in front of the chair. They look familiar. He begins to see the marks more clearly. Can those be blissymbols? he thinks to himself. He looks at Aletheia.

So, you recognize them.

I think so. Epoché pauses. Can you read them?

I can write them! Aletheia smiles.

Where did they…unearth? He thought blissymbols were extinct.

I had a visitor earlier who left them for me.

Epoché now realizes their strategy must change. We'll have to go to the temporary autonomous zones right away. Do you think our instruments are sensitive enough? he asks.

Aletheia paces around the chair. Possibly. But I must cipher the narrative once again. I'm working on it now. Now I'm the one sounding global!

In the distance, the ocean and horizon are almost entirely dark with no delineating line between them.

Shared Axiom

Both are begging to be reset. She seeks the animal inside her who goes deeper, and she lets him—

When we were talking about light we were talking about love. We learned that an electron can couple with ∞, and that each event (a note, a chord) suggests a continuation along the borderlines of repetition, what might be called *narrative capacity*. When an *a-quark* couples with a *b-quark* in the poem, emitting a function for ∞, can the couple then couple with the resulting bombarding diversity, what might be thought of as their magnetic moment?

And what about the function of *narrative capacity* on the modeling of DNA as extraterrestrial, or when painting the ribboning coils of DNA closer to the substrate, where they change form to better fit the substrate while developing a new ∞ coupling, as if the DNA notes (chords) are infinitely divisible and therefore of infinite size? Does the molecular spacing expand so that the inner core of ∞ resists inertia? Maybe, except in the case of the coupling ∞, where a particle takes the place of the ordinary = intuitive function, shielding every stellar flare, body pulse, coronal loop. The particle in such conditions outlives normative matter, preventing the momentum of the particle in time-reversable manifolds and creating ramifications for the resulting ghost matter: the reader reading, the light on light.

As a result, light particles, which have relativistic speeds, would be impervious to the formation of new matter, which is needed to increase the longevity of virtual particles, or what could be thought of as ambiguous relations between the text and word.

Back in the earliest moments of cosmic history, the beginning of the poem was also its end, the accompanying suns also neutrinos, the anticharmed hydrons threshold stimuli.

Love was a light and perhaps even likely.

But the sun does not have enough angular momentum to break up its burns. All practical observations of the behavior of matter can be reduced, with the user—the reader or author—deciding which information is needed to discover the poem's underlying genetic code, what might be thought of as the author-in-the-text.

An open system in this context is both a closed system and a grand theory, all differing eccentricities in which electrons have the same *narrative capacity* for orgasm. Here, when physical quantities become infinite in a theory, even in a theory of narration, it means that something (an *a-quark*, a *b-quark*) has diverged from the quest toward unification.

Thus, the equation, the image, the story, or the poem that has at its degenerate era a coupling ∞ expresses its orbital path as if such a path is taking place in a solar system—character-planets revolving around a story-sun. Which is to say that the solar system as a controlling conceit for the body might be more useful to the coupling ∞ as a function of astronomical space ≠ its subatomic counterpart in molecular space.

Either way, love is a poem always changing its character, a coupling ∞ colliding with the lightest of elements—hydrogen, a touch of lithium—its notes and chords exhibiting from a radial, shifting point of density, where the heaviest elements, like sex, produce a value that is greater than a number that can be imagined in the poem, and, most especially, outside of it.

Therefore, when it comes to predicting the shape of the multiverse = the book, we must first acknowledge that such a shape would transcend its immediate coupling capacity and is only partially contingent on its *a-quarks* and *b-quarks* and their ∞ coupling.

More directly, the shape of the multiverse = book is dependent on the way in which its geometry of spacetime is curved: positively, as in a sphere; negatively, as in a saddle; zero, as in flat; or curved the way bodies wrap and wet. If simultaneously coiled through positive, negative, flat, or curved spacetime, the shape of the multiverse = book might be said to propagate the spatial relationships between characters, between the *narrative capacities* of its aesthetics. Saying that the multiverse = book has a shape is much like saying that love has a story, which it does sometimes, though its story deforms the narrative toward a broadening event horizon.

Love is like curving. It is both the shape of the curve and the curve itself. The characters are the eyelets of the author and the authors themselves. The setting is the ∞ coupling of the quarks and the quarks never observed. The multiverse = book is the acceleration of a Big Bang toward expansion and expansion itself, the multiple orgasms that roll and roll. Its *narrative capacity* is the idealized coil of the poem and the coil uncoiling and coiling. At present time, all are coupling—

Indefinite Resonance

Earlier, Epoché had followed the faint veins of roads winding up the mountain in the distance, inhaling the brilliant air, undiminished, the end of a chain.

He saw what the river looked like under its skin. He saw what he looked like under the river's skin.

I am writing to you at the edge of things called distances, he thinks.

The birds continue in flight. These birds, he says, using his fingers to make wings.

Once he used the *iEpiphany* to make contact with Aletheia, he began working on another translation. Below its surface opacity something seemed to speak to him, a shipwrecked echo of the book, a glittering SOS. The sand eventually eroded the grassy dunes. This approach, to translate himself out of context, was just what he needed to make the necessary leaps.

The Dial

Aletheia was making the final adjustments. I would like to be one and many and none, she chants, clicking the arrows into place.

This, she says, will make us never forget. This one will stop the war. This one, all wars. Click, click.

This one...she pauses. She studies the arrow, shiny and sharp. This one, she thinks, will keep us as mutable as the clouds.

This is the Value of Inquiry

Since blissymbols were a plausible language to some but not all, the visitor went to the library.

Something replicated.
Undressed.
Features were examined.
Some petals grew into portals.
But the visitor did not stop at symmetry.
Not this time.
Rare results were produced.
But the visitor needed something else.
That would work day or night.
Change on its own.
And keep up.
In clumps.
Sometimes legibly.

Like organs, some were internal.
They grew larger.
Into scales.
One scale was blue. Another orange.
Some flames were green.
Lakes.
Still others were without color.
And others with all.

His favorite color was the vowel.
Her favorite vowel was the atom.
His favorite atom was the rhythm.
Her favorite rhythm was the prism.
His favorite prism was the violet.
Her favorite violet was the lyric.
His favorite lyric was the logic.
Her favorite logic was the toxic.
His favorite toxic was the vertex.
Her favorite vertex was the tonic.
His favorite tonic was the cortex.

To the visitor's delight, it seemed to be working. The ocean was getting louder.
Aletheia and Epoché would soon arrive.

Temporary Autonomous Zones

Temporary autonomous zones—TAZ as they are affectionately called—are forged rather than entered. In TAZ there are options to get to a point. Activity scallops, an afterlife of the experiment. One upcoming chapter argues for telling the difference.

In TAZ the practice of framing a rule as a ruin makes even more ruins, as anyone familiar with the latest studies has been informed.

The rule with a positive amplitude cancels a ruin with a negative amplitude simply by exciting the atom. Some atoms are mosaics. It is the role of the player in TAZ to decide whether to follow or ignore the walkthrough.

Additional poems will be played in TAZ.

Will the player be played backward?

Will the player enter the fortress equipped with money or fantasy?

Will hungry avatars use the players to intervene in the doctrine?

Is there a feasible, yet risky, rescue plan?

Can repositioning the poem solve the puzzle?

Rules ask even more of the players they compute.

For example, I work to explain the folly of the refutation of technology. Normally, privately, I wonder if it is a dramatic slip of the pen...

Such idealism in TAZ is unavoidable. One cannot help but marvel at the delicate indentations left over from the migratory meteors. Much of the fascination with cultural memory in TAZ is that the language in the center chambers can adhere to any structure, including itself and the witness. Its future position and momentum cannot be known with certainty because its present conditions cannot be known without ambiguity. In TAZ the starting atmospheric conditions cannot be measured.

A new rule is formed.

Free Will

As one operative against the war, the visitor thought of itself as a nonconformist. Subconsciously, the visitor was all electricity, deranged and vast. As an architect of space, its books were immaculate. The visitor arranged them like honeycombs, synapses firing past speeds of light.

It is unthinkable, the visitor muses. How can I not join them? But I will have to give myself a name.

No one in TAZ was aware that the visitor had many names. It was just a matter of choosing.

The Enduring Karmanaut

When I was born, I was a letter delivered by the sea in a ship crafted with no limit for travel. My fingerprint unlocked a supercivilization behind my throat. My cells write without sight. The ship sailed between the horizon and the sea to the land where I was born. I was born into a letter. My fingerprint was found by a supercivilization. When I was born, the sea unlocked a horizon behind my throat. My paradox will be wider than my cell.

Questionairre

All around TAZ, crowds gathered and glowed. Word had spread of Aletheia and Epoché's arrival.

If we could see the wave function of a person, someone says.

If we could chart our psychological constellations, Aletheia proposes. Epoché stands like an autobiography beside her. The Enduring Karmanaut steps out from the crowd, welcoming them.

Are you content with your choice, then? Aletheia asks the Enduring Karmanaut.

Yes, the Enduring Karmanaut says. I was born of letters. My paradox is wider than my cell.

Relieved, Aletheia begins the sequence.

At first the crowds gasp, then cheer. They weren't used to seeing previously censored signs performed so freely. Aletheia considers the tides that carry her thoughts home. Here, she would need a different conduit.

She unwraps the ancient telescope from a sturdy cloth. Except that it doesn't look like a telescope. Aletheia modified most of its parts.

Aletheia looks at Epoché and the Enduring Karmanaut. They nod. We are ready, then, she says, putting the arrows into place.

Click, click.

Gone are the crowds, the crumbling ruins. Opening our eyes to something else. An absolute system.

Mock-Heroic

For the people living at the base of the tomb where the war began like all wars begin where the first troops of the war landed where the war placed its greatest assets at the base of the tomb where the war digs into the land like a dying soldier and the nonsoldiers enter the wars outside the war that no one is fighting because we are inside fighting a war where the war and its wars are like a new war where the war grows at the base of the tomb where the victims grow inside the tomb where there is naming to be done since the naming of the war and the naming of all wars was a name to name and the war and its unnamed wars landed at the base of the tomb where the war began like all wars and where both soldier and nonsoldier must transform themselves to delete it.

The Novella

The first person to read the novella is distraught. As if it narrates our war. I don't think we are at war. But I rewrite the novella so no one will cry.

War Novella

Much later I think, maybe the novella is a war novella a war novella a war
NOVELLA A WAR NOVELLA WAR NOVELLA WAR NOVELLA WAR
NOVELLA WAR NOVELLA A WAR A NOVELLA A WAR NOVELLA A
WAR NOVELLA WAR NOVELLA OF WAR NOVELLA OF WAR A WAR
NOVELLA WAR NOVELLA WAR NOVELLA OF WAR A WAR NOVELLA
WAR NOVELLA WAR NOVELLA WAR NOVELLA WAR NOVELLA WAR
NOVELLA WAR NOVELLA WAR NOVELLA WAR NOVELLA WAR
NOVELLA WAR NOVELLA OF WAR NOVELLA WAR NOVELLA WAR
NOVELLA WAR NOVELLA WAR NOVELLA WAR NOVELLA A WAR
NOVELLA OF WAR A WAR NOVELLA NO WAR NO WAR NO WAR
NO WAR NO WAR NO WAR NO WAR NO NOVELLA WAR NOVELLA
WAR NOVELLA WAR NOVELLA WAR NOVELLA WARN NO WARN OF
WAR WAR NO WAR NO WAR NO WAR NO WAR NO WAR NO WAR
WARN WARN WARN WARN OF WAR O WAR NO WAR NOVELLA NO
NOVELLA WAR NOVELLA NO NO NO WAR NO WAR NO WAR WAR
NO WAR O WAR O WAR O NO NO WAR NO WAR NO WAR WAR O WAR

NOVELLA WAR NO WAR NOVELLA NO WAR WAR WAR WAR WAR
NOVELLA WAR NO NO WAR NOVELLA NO WAR WAR WAR WAR
NO WAR NO NO NO NO NO NO NO NO NO NO NO NO NO NO NO
NO NO NO NO NO NO NO NO NO NO NO NO NO NO NO NO
NO NO NO NO NO NO NO NO NO NO NO NO NO NO NO NO
NO NO NO NO NO NO NO NO NO NO NO NO NO NO NO NO
NO NO NO NO NO NO NO NO NO NO NO NO NO NO NO NO
NO NO NO NO NO NO NO NO NO NO NO NO NO NO NO NO
NO NO NO NO NO NO NO NO NO NO NO NO NO NO NO NO
NO NO NO NO NO NO NO NO NO NO NO NO NO NO NO NO
NO NO NO NO NO NO NO NO NO NO NO NO NO NO NO NO
NO NO NO NO NO NO NO NO NO NO NO NO NO NO NO NO
NO NO NO NO NO NO NO NO NO NO NO NO NO NO NO NO
NO NO NO NO NO NO NO NO NO NO NO NO NO NO NO NO
NO NO NO NO NO NO NO NO NO NO NO NO NO NO NO NO NO
NO NO NO NO NO NO NO NO NO NO NO NO NO NO NO NO
NO NO NO NO NO NO NO NO NO NO NO NO NO NO NO NO
NO NO NO NO NO NO NO NO NO NO NO NO NO NO NO NO
NO NO NO NO NO NO NO NO NO NO NO NO NO NO NO NO
NO NO NO NO NO NOW WE ARE AT WAR NO NO NOW WE ARE AT
WAR NO NO NOW WE ARE AT WAR NO NO NOW WE ARE AT WAR
NO NO NOW WE ARE AT WAR NO NO NOW WE ARE AT WAR NO
NO NOW WE ARE AT WAR NO NO NO NO NOW WE ARE AT WAR

NOW NOW NOW NOW NOW NO NO NO NOW NOW NO NO NO NO
NOW NOW NOW NOW NOW NOW NOW NOW NOW NOW NOW
NOW NOW WE ARE AT WAR NO NO NOW WE ARE AT WAR NO NO
NOW WE ARE AT WAR NO NO NOW WE ARE AT WAR NO NO NOW
WE ARE AT WAR NO NO NOW WE ARE AT WAR NO NO NOW WE
ARE AT WAR NO NO NOW WE ARE AT WAR NO NO NOW WE ARE
AT WAR NO NO NOW WE ARE AT WAR NO NO NOW WE ARE AT
WAR NO NO NOW WE ARE AT WAR NO NO NOW WE ARE AT WAR
NO NO NOW WE ARE AT WAR NO NO NOW WE ARE AT WAR NO
NO NOW WE ARE AT WAR NO NO NOW WE ARE AT WAR NO NO
NOW WE ARE AT WAR NO NO NOW WE ARE AT WAR NO NO NOW
WE ARE AT WAR NO NO NOW WE ARE AT WAR NO NO NOW WE
ARE AT WAR NO NOW WE ARE AT WAR WAR WAR WAR WAR WAR
WAR WAR WAR WAR WAR WAR WAR WAR WAR WAR WAR WAR
WAR WAR WAR WAR WAR WAR WAR WAR WAR WAR WAR WAR
WAR WAR WAR WAR WAR WAR WAR WAR WAR WAR WAR WAR
WAR WAR WAR WAR WAR WAR WAR WAR WAR WAR WAR WAR
WAR WAR WAR WAR WAR WAR WAR WAR WAR WAR WAR WAR
WAR WAR WAR WAR WAR WAR WAR WAR WAR WAR WAR WAR
WAR WAR WAR WAR WAR WAR WAR WAR WAR WAR WAR WAR
WAR WAR WAR WAR WAR WAR WAR WAR WAR WAR WAR WAR
WAR WAR WAR WAR WAR WAR WAR WAR WAR WAR WAR WAR
WAR WAR WAR WAR WAR WAR WAR WAR WAR WAR WAR
WAR WAR WAR WAR WAR WAR WAR WAR WAR WAR WAR WAR
WAR WAR WAR WAR WAR NO NO NO NO NO NO NO NO NO NO NO

NO NO NO NO NO NO NO NO NO NO NO WAR WAR WAR WAR WAR
WAR WAR WAR NO NO NO NO NO NO NO NO NO NO NO WAR WAR
WAR WAR WAR WAR WAR NO NO NO WAR WAR WAR WAR WAR
WAR WAR WAR WAR WAR WAR WAR WAR WAR WAR WAR WAR
WAR WAR WAR WAR WAR WAR WAR WAR WAR WAR WAR WAR
WAR WAR WAR WAR WAR WAR WAR WAR WAR WAR WAR WAR
WAR WAR WAR WAR WAR WAR WAR WAR WAR WAR WAR WAR
WAR WAR WAR WAR WAR WAR WAR WAR WAR WAR WAR WAR
WAR WAR WAR WAR WAR WAR WAR WAR WAR WAR WAR WAR
WAR WAR WAR NO WAR WAR WAR WAR WAR WAR WAR WAR WAR
WAR WAR WAR WAR WAR WAR WAR WAR WAR WAR WAR WAR WAR
WAR WAR WAR NO WAR WAR WAR WAR WAR WAR WAR WAR WAR
WAR WAR NO WAR WAR WAR WAR WAR WAR NO WAR NO WAR NO
NO WAR WAR WAR WAR WAR WAR WAR NO WAR NO WAR NO NO
NO WAR NO NO NO WAR NO WAR NO WAR NO WAR NO WAR NO
NO NO NO NO NO NO NO NO NO NO NO NO NO NO NO NO
NO NO NO NO NO NO NO NO NO NO NO NO NO NO NO NO
NO NO NO NO NO NO NO NO NO NO NO NO NO NO NO NO
NO NO NO NO NO NO NO NO NO NO NO NO NO NO NO NO
NO NO NO NO NO NO NO NO NO NO NO NO NO NO NO NO
THE NOVELLA IS IS IS IS IS IS IS IS IS IS IS IS NOT A NOVELLA THE
NOVELLA IS IS IS IS IS IS IS IS IS IS IS IS IS IS IS IS IS IS IS IS IS IS IS
IS IS IS IS IS IS IS IS IS IS ISIS ISIS ISIS ISIS ISIS ISIS ISIS ISIS ISIS ISIS
ISIS ISIS IS IS IS IS IS IS ISIS ISIS ISIS ISIS ISIS ISIS ISIS ISIS ISIS ISIS

ISISSSSSSSSSSSSSSSSSSSSSSSSSSSSSSSSSSSSSSSSSSSSSSSSSSSSSSSSSS
SSSSSSSSSSSSSSSSSSSSSSSSSSSSSSSSSSSSSSSSSSSSSSSSSSSSSSSSSSSS
SSSSSSSSSSSSSSSSSSSSSSSSSSSSSSSSSSSSSSSSSSSSSSSSSSSSSSSSSSSS
SSSSSSSSSSSSSSSSSSSSSSSSSSSSSSSSSSSSSSSSSSSSSSSSSSSSSSSSSSSS
SSSSSSSSSSSSSSSSSSSSSSSSSSSSSSSSSSSSSSSSSSSSSSSSSSSSSSSSSSSS
SSSSSSSSSSSSSSSSSSSSSSSSSSSSSSSSSSSSSSSSSSSSSSSSSSSSSSSSSSSS
SSSSSSSSSSSSSSSSSSSSSSSSSSSSSSSSSSSSSSSSSSSSSSSSSSSSSSSSSSSS
SSSSSSSSSSSSSSSSSSSSSSSSSSSSSSSSSSSSSSSSSSSSSSSSSSSSSSSSSSSS
SSSSSSSSSSSSSSSSSSSSSSSSSSSSSSSSSSSSSSSSSSSSSSSSSSSSSSSSSSSS
SSSSSSSSSSSSSSSSSSSSSSSSSSSSSSSSSSSSSSSSSSSSSSSSSSSSSSSSSSSS
SSSSSSSSSSSSSSSSSSSSSSSSSSSSSSSSSSSSSSSSSSSSSSSSSSSSSSSSSSSS
SSSSSSSSSSSSSSSSSSSSSSSSSSSSSSSSSSSSSSSSSSSSSSSSSSSSSSSSSSSS
SSSSSSSSSSSSSSSSSSSSSSSSSSSSSSSSSSSSSSSSSSSSSSSSSSSSSSSSSSSS
SSSSSSSSSSSSSSSSSSSSSSSSSSSSSSSSSSSSSSSSSSSSSSSSSSSSSSSSSSSS
SSSSSSSSSSSSSSSSSSSSSSSSSSSSSSSSSSSSSSSSSSSSSSSSSSSSSSSSSSSS
SSSSSSSSSSSSSSSSSSSSSSSSSSSSSSSSSSSSSSSSSSSSSSSSSSSSSSSSSSSS
SSSSSSSSSSSSSSSSSSSSSSSSSSSSSSSSSSSSSSSSSSSSSSSSSSSSSSSSSSSS
SSSSSSSSSSSSSSSSSSSSSSSSSSSSSSSSSSSSSSSSSSSSSSSSSSSSSSSSSSSS
SSSSSSSSSSSSSSSSSSSSSSSSSSSSSSSSSSSSSSSSSSSSSSSSSSSSSSSSSSSS
SSSSSSSSSSSSSSSSSSSSSSSSSSSSSSSSSSSSSSSSSSSSSSSSSSSSSSSSSSSS
SSSSSSSSSSSSSSSSSSSSSSSSSSSSSSSSSSSSSSSSSSSSSSSSSSSSSSSSSSSS
SSSSSSSSSSSSSSSSSSSSSSSSSSSSSSSSSSSSSSSSSSSSSSSSSSSSSSSSSSSS
SSSSSSSSSSSSSSSSSSSSSSSSSSSSSSSSSSSSSSSSSSSSSSSSSSSSSSSSSSSS

O War

Eleven Asteroids (Dimensions)

the project ignited versions
of itself. modifications were made
for the sake of "accuracy." like a veil
like an actual chain reaction.

I stayed there for a while like that.
      could my navigation be taken
in. the spine of the ship I
fly in and out of view.

between the subject and object—
that old tale—lies the earliest
instabilities. stuffed in uniforms
we witness the transfer ripples.

like the aftershock fuel across
                    from me. into everything you
            think the printed boundary is a
    fullbody opening for the sign.

this elsewhere a limitless act.
                the inlet and moon solids.
        shall I relinquish the spheres
so the shore moves forward.

in the future we like to imagine
       things propel us. I am changing
   the mast. so that the widest cuts
of the sky are more easily defined.

while allowing for the possibility of
simultaneity we view
waves as words. all choices
require accentuated accents.

to make gravitation more concrete I
ornament its trusted surface.
with a vocabulary or a galaxy
humidly entering the currents.

is one consequence that language
        wherever it is becomes our hero.
like us it lives. deranging the output
where anterior triggers aperture.

you would know this if you were
             not a question to be displayed.
         if you were not a question like
     us, bit by bit, baring arias.

Theory of Tides

Aletheia, Epoché, and the Enduring Karmanaut entered the war. Some said the war entered them. When they returned, they spent much of the transition together.

Adaptive, this anarchy is not conditional but contextual. Like waves interacting with an incoming wave. The water gets deeper as the tide approaches the land, slowing down the wave. But since the edge of the land is irregular, the slowing of the wave is irregular.

Which is why your extrasensory lighthouse signal, Aletheia writes.

As if right now reading between the slow ripples in a pond. I reply.

We were willing to roam the waters as tidal waves with momentum, attached yet unhitched. On the bank of the pond where you and I create tests. To determine what shape will the sea be? What shape will we be?

Aftermaths/Beginnings

Under   the constellation o   f showy ou w hy they stood a   side the

a   g g r e g a t e, a b a n d   one   d, be   long   i n g t o a

n   y set— We   called f o r t h   the system to   resume

o f f c o u r s e.   Tessellating I   drew then   c   licked   start to

star   t. Taken off the   finger   on e petal   at a t i m e I f

ell apart reading the time   table asking   how can   that be? How

can t   he knot undo   the   rope & how can   the   rope undo

the ode when   the novella knots?   I know wh   at   orbits ins   side the orb   it.   T   the harmony   of

s p h e r e s r e l e   as   e s t h e e s c   ape hatch   of   what

might be called infinities—sh   all I?—a r e s h e l l g a   m e   s.

The i   mages   used to re   create   them are symbols t

hat at   tempt to re   present.   This works   well enough

in   practice,   but   after   time   time   i s under

stood   to be a   weather   comma   n d i n g t h   e butterfly e missions   of all out l i n e s, t h e s e a ' s   most   probable

moons   t   ones.   You   are   being encouraged   to rush

through   the   chapter's   proto   c o l f u l l s c r e e n

with the   i d e a of the moon   delayed,   and to

do   s o a t a n y h   our, or on   any   day.   Now,

when t h e s e a   deciphers   letters   instead   of

the element   s, l i p s s p e l l o u t the   symbol f   or   lyre:

looveloeloelovovelovovelovlovlveloloeloelo
ovloelolovloeovelveoveovelovlveveoveloeel
veloeovelovovelovlovveoveloeelveoveveov
oveveoveloelvelvelovlveloloeoovelolveov
velvelovlovlveovelelovovelovlooveelveelv
elvovlvelovoolveloellovlloelveoveloellve ov
elvelveloeloeloelovovelovlovlovlovloeoveo
veoveloeelvelveovelveloloulveloelovlovlvelovl
vellovlovlovlovloelvelveloelvelvlveovelovl
oeoveloelolveloeoveovelovveovelelveloeove
llovoveoveoveoveloelovovelolaeveoveovelv
elvelovlvelveloelovlovlololavoveloeovelelaeo
velveveveovelveloelveloelvelovlovlvevveleloelvelo

Predicated

on the
    gathering exit
       we are pleated by
            our
            narrowest
            arrows
                tucked into fanning
                    pirouettes

To the Unaided Eye

Like memory loss and its anti-matter, unabridged. In a moment for eight hours. Accepting its astronomical weight at the bottom of the clear sea like an unstoppable anchor.

You say to me several times, and I hear nothing but one. Then I hear nothing, but I know something was said.

I propose this.

You hear what I said and then forget it.

I say. The memory of having spoken.

You respond in capital letters.

I await messages, documents. Moving the ocean beneath me, still sunk.

I repeat.

Equal and opposite a mirror contains simultaneous worlds. A single false flag or not one at all. A national flag or a personal flag made from seasonal flowers to make a point about impermanence.

She says. Moving beneath her.

I swim to shore.

A type of literary archeology, the books I love all contain timelines of the history of

I prefer to keep current.
I work my mouth.
Dreaming in crop circles.
I mistake voice-overs.
For favors.
I am fond of.
Satin/spirals.
I disregard.
Pseudo/citation.
I often point.
To supermassive.
Black holes.
Vaguely.
Perhaps suddenly.
Sensing.
My characters.
Monologuing.
Landscaping.
Overlapping.
…Au contraire…
Symbolically.

I succumb.
As if here is where.
I chalk-outline my speech.
I mean memorize.
Object.
Devote/disrobe.
I am beside myself.
With biota.
Bloodbonds.
Dorsalwave.
Glossaries.
Secretly.
I flinch.
My wings.
Paperless.
I make my entrance.

The air bubbles rise to the surface. I can't seem to escape the memory of how many fingers am I holding up? Carefully modulated our thoughts are traveling by sonar through waves broadcasting a new world order.

Today, buried in the stargrave, I light special tools to find my way. My other senses are sharpened. But your candor stays with me. Changes me. Even down here. Which is why all of this—This!—is not simply a deconstruction of fine delicacies.

Someone is finding and losing my way through the thicket of things. Emerging into notes I play that lightning on. Twice.

I've seen it and lived through its sideways mastery.

Let There Be Love

She lives in one of the crystal petals of the constellation.

In a wing she called starfish.

And in the multiple arms, or bodies when her eyes were open, along with all the others of the stone sea.

The sky, a hundred mirrors, sets once every ten days until the eleventh day when it grows.

The waves came in lost languages.

The starfish looked like a country.

The official version omitted everything that didn't glow.

She lives on the borderland, which is itself one of the feathers on the wing.

She uses the pink most frequently but also indigo and a dreaming blue.

The collarbone is always made from the most delicate shells, having been collected from long walks holding hands in the novella.

She enjoys creature comforts, handmade shawls made from unspeakable patterns back when the costume designers were open for business.

Every window is decorated with her favorite planet.

The planets spin between worlds as worlds.

The wing is spinning toward someone else's window; her favorite planet dissolves.

When she wakes, the planets wake, too.

The sun moves easily through the stone sea; it flies assuredly through the mirror sky.

It hovers over skyscrapers.

People drop pearls from their eyes.

She picks up the pearls and drives to the sea, where she tries to skip them like rocks. They roll in her hands, collapse into the waves, get caught in the crevices, vanish down impossible fissures…

They coalesce under the water in luminous patches.

After several months people go to look for their pearls. They begin with day trips but eventually stay overnight in the undersea reefs.

Each person is an explorer.

Innumerable discoveries are made.

Some discoveries are made into lockets.

Some prompt people to move.

Some discoveries heal the passage of time, but then another discovery is made, and time is thought to be without passage.

Some discoveries take years to accept.

Some are immediately forgotten.

Some are offered to friends as something else.

Some are only visible above the sea.

Some discoveries exist for just a moment.
Some make exploring easier, faster, more fulfilling.
Some can be whatever you want.
I am reading one now.

Hotwired Blue Wire

Thus the laws of cause and effect become the myths upon which the worlds are built. Flowers are transformed into nature's own sculptures and machinery into the metaphorical expression of prose. The concept of belief is contingent upon objective standards, closely associated with degrees of truth that rely on assumptions, as if subjective experience constitutes lived experience. Right away a correlation is made between sensory experience and the physical world. Existence itself cannot be adequately accounted for by an inorganic world-view. Natural instincts are thought to be governed at an unconscious or pre-rational level. These moments cannot be translated. The mechanized world is described so that it commodifies lived experience. Human agency soon comes into play. The speaker wonders whether or not we are instinctively aware of our own agency, our own mindfulness, beyond objectively based barometers. Epistemological concerns are explored within an old dichotomy. Philosophy, like science and religion, is equated with an objective worldview and put at odds with the natural world. The speaker tries to make a case for the positions of both objective and subjective knowledge, then claims these can coexist in timelessness; an instant fixed would approach the infinite. While the speaker entertains the idea that these two polarized forms of knowledge can coexist within one worldview, the speaker argues for the validity of lived experience over objectively based knowledge. The speaker's attack on objectivity continues, for the apparent objective world outside of the self, what is characterized as the other, is once again rejected. Within the speaker's argument for the personal worldview, the self as an agent becomes the ordering principle from which lived experience is measured.

Hotwired Red Wire

The speaker denies each object's essence or thingness as a substance that exists independently in the world. The notion of an object failing to exist as a thing-in-itself is presented by a sentence that tonally sounds like the first premise to a syllogism. Substance is greater in value and meaning than its particulars. An atomistic explanation of essence is described. The relation of each entity to the other is given priority over the essence of each entity in itself. The term "while" signifies a temporal connection between two disparate things. Continuity is differentiated from the sameness of objects. The self as a possible entity or more than a sign that signifies a referent is characterized as being different from an intentional object or a process of communication. The alliteration of the soft "s" sound is juxtaposed with the cautionary rhetoric about the similarity between self and sign. The image makes the objects invisible rather than merely similar. Appearance, the objects turned invisible, is contrasted with actuality, the objects as things prior to their invisibility. The lack of physical appearance operates within a different category altogether than the objects that share sameness, for invisibility, as a descriptive device, is radically different than sameness as a quality. The repetition of the soft "c" and "s" sounds, as well as the two hard "t" sounds, provide a counterbalance to the relational nature of the diction. The line sings. Objects in the world are suspect of being substances in the same way dreams are suspect. Similar to the word "while," the word "or" connects two paradoxical statements about physical origin. If it is possible to come from one place and also another, then these two places must exist as the same thing, unless they are part of a larger dreaming. The description, therefore, lies in the disappearance from the sky, in the movement away from an open sky, in the metaphorical view of clarity. A subjective syntax appears to follow the form of thought in the mind: first the image itself is given and then the act of attention on the image. Two somatic clauses are unified with the use of a comma, evoking another possible consequence to the urge of letting memory speak. In one assertion, the subject-object relationship is conceptualized hierarchically, as if the interests of the self are delegated to the interests of the other. In the other, image or representation is consistently available for witness.

L'informe

discursive dreams

with depth

as inside

dreams with

thrust—

a book

of pinholes

confirms

the result

nonstop

I

identify

fortunes

in the

petals

like an atlas stretched

to

translucency—

flashing gems like badges

the chiral titles

of these oceans—

The Belief in Elementary Particles

You were going to tell me, what was it that you dreamt? the Enduring Karmanaut reminds Epoché.

I guess it's more like how than what, Epoché responds. He presses the pedal to accelerate.

What if it's more like why than how, Aletheia chimes in. She inspects the map. We take a soft right here.

Epoché swings into the swerve.

Why do we dream? the Enduring Karmanaut repeats, stretching back in the seat.

Ἀλήθεια καὶ Ἐποχή

We are always being changed by the war. But we aren't always sure how. We sometimes distinguish ourselves before the war. And who I have become after the war, Epoché explains. But the middle—Epoché pauses—the middle is almost entirely absent—

Well then we are dreaming the middle, aren't we all? Aletheia remarks.

That's the thing. We cannot distinguish ourselves between the beginning the middle the end or in which direction.

I just know that the war grew at the base of the tomb.

I know that we went there to stop a war.

We went to the base of the tomb.

We tried to stop the war by making names.

We named the war and even more wars.

We made more names, and in doing so, we tried to unname the war.

Our names deleted us.

We translated our names.

Our names are symbols.

We tried to stop the war by creating names—as many names as the stars.
Our language is starlight.
We travel in all directions.
We let our names change, so that when the war approaches, we can ask:

what

is your name?

what

have we begun

to use

as

names?

The Origin of the Work of Art

When I began reading poems they began reading me. I turned back through the book to the chapter of thinking, for we want to know what this reminds us of: expanding, ablaze, letting the sun shine through.

To write yourself into the history of others.

And they write themselves like emancipators into you.

Making it possible by adding elaborate maps, the long windmill nights, before I realized we were altering

Matter, like we alter our belief in tomorrow, where the blues meet in the sky on their own terms. Surfaces part, waves spread. The atom as we know it splits not just itself but the years, too.

I make from the book a canopy of peace to show most directly what is missing.

One of my optics, I think you can extract it, it's a proposition to a proposition.

So that when we say the word *sky* we mean *gathering a sky* to establish its breadth as a great and luminous equalizer.

It also seems to be a love story entering itself by performance.

Houses and trees and plumes from clouds trickle off. Something similar occurs when I follow my own astronomy, willful yet unconscious.

Gleefully I watch for the fireworks mishaps. Facing the electricity I see in my future, I sit and watch the bees under their burden, sympathetic, cautious, months might pass.

And in the meantime I have written you out of space. I request that you come and visit, say hello, tell me what your status is as a comet, tell me precisely how did you cross the lacework in the atmosphere's border? Did they let you take anything along—something to remind you of your trajectory?

Until branches spill over that monolith:

memory

global

positioning

wired

labyrinth

relative

diction

distinct

beauty

fiction

fiction my

novel

accessory

Sailing to the End of the World

And to the beginning of a new one, Epoché says, his eyes almost capsizing, keeping the ship afloat. Aletheia staggers as she cross examines the waves. The Enduring Karmanaut practices a private palmistry, reading the ocean's heart, head, fate, and lifelines. All attempts at overt communication.

Variegated Passages

The book is like a sieve, she replies.

It is like a sieve.

It is like a submerged sieve.

It floats, Aletheia reminds, even below water.

That is clear.

It is a fact.

That is correct.

It appears so.

This is also my take on it.

This does, in fact, appear to be the case.

I believe so.

You speak with clarity.

Hmmm.

Yes, indeed.

That is absolutely the case.

It is clear, Epoché says.

Correct.

It is like a sieve.

I think this is the case, more than all of you.

Very right.

That is doubtlessly correct.

That is correct, I would think.

Of course.

Of course it is.

Absolutely, without a doubt.

Without a doubt in my mind.

We all know it, the Enduring Karmanaut says.

It is absolutely clear.

This is the way it could be, you propose.

But how can that be so?

How can it be otherwise?

What now?

What?

The book is a sieve.

With transparent seams.

Communiqué

No, listen, this is what happened: I was looking for this thing, Aletheia. That's right. Pushing through the fresh air, to which Aletheia seems accustomed, the fresh air and the indiscriminate waves outside like recitatives, or are those memes?

Under some circumstances, Aletheia says.

This time I respond above water.

I say watch it because the water ahead of us and behind us and even under us keeps sliding away; only the moons are left. We expect that from above us, but from every side?

At the very least, what I want to say is that I was looking for this thing by purposefully letting it seek me out. It found me one day as I was developing a different stratagem.

Epoché was named in close proximity. The visitor had found me; that part is obvious. Once named, the Enduring Karmanaut crouched like an animal nearby, ear to the ground.

I don't usually feel the continental drift happening below. But tonight it jarred me awake like the approach of something building. Luckily this world is a sphere. So we'll be prepared for any surprise encounters when sailing all the way to the edge.

Can you imagine it? Aletheia asks. If you just dropped off?

AUTHOR'S STATEMENT: AN ARTIFICIAL INTELLIGENCE

One of my favorite things about relativity is that matter causes a curvature of spacetime in its immediate vicinity. I imagine all of reality warped but in grassroots scales. My writing is full of wishful thinking.

Consequently, I might describe the authorial intent in *Starlight in Two Million: A Neo-Scientific Novella* as quantum jumping between intention and non-intention. However, if authorial intent is a psycho-linguistic phenomenon, or if the content, form, and/or contexts of literary works can present arguments that are counter to an author's goals, Authorial Intent might be better recognized as an Artificial Intelligence, its own kind of fiction...

Or data plan? If so, here is a version of the plan:

One of my aims in this project is to experiment with point of view by developing a question—"Is there a 4th person narration?"—posed by Shanxing Wang in his book, *Mad Science in Imperial City* (Futurepoem, 2005). In physics, which can be defined as the study of physical reality, the fourth dimension of space is time. In the context of string theory, where our universe is thought to be one of a wilderness of universes comprised of infinite dimensions of space and time that are made up of vibrating membranes of energy known as open and closed strings, I imagine 4th person narration as a site for considering narrative mode in relation to higher-dimensions in physical reality. (The arrow of time is a circle; it just does not know it. What the circle does not know is that it is a hypercube.) Applying principles in theoretical physics and other sciences to the composition and interpretation of literary works is part of my investigation into *quantum poetics*, a hybrid critical-speculative framework that I am extending upon and developing in this project and others.

I envision 4th person narration as operating at both the astronomical scale of narration and the subatomic scale of the sentence in the creative texts that I reference in the novella's epigraphs—Wang's *Mad Science in Imperial City*, Laura Moriarty's novel, *Ultravioleta* (Atelos, 2005), and the work of Alfred Jarry (1873–1907). To intentionally and/or unintentionally engage in a narrative mode within or beyond the fourth dimension might be to read, write, or construct texts outside of time, or in all times, making nonlinearity and simultaneity points of view and spacetime a literary device.

Similar phenomena can be seen in the visual language of Vance Kirkland (1904–1981), whose cosmological "Dot Paintings"/Energy in Space Abstractions, with their simultaneous foregrounding of micro and macro scales, have inspired my experiments with point of view. Kirkland's *Four Suns in Space*, used for the novella's front and back cover, is mesmerizing in its pulsing hyperboles. I especially admire how Kirkland, a synaesthete, made it and other paintings by strapping himself horizontally in a contraption so that he was suspended above the canvas, pressing down dowels dipped in paint for each stroke. Sometimes we must subvert our gravitational pull to paint what we want. Additionally, the red suns in the painting remind me of "barbelith," an image of a red circle that is used repeatedly and variably by Grant Morrison in his comic book series, *The Invisibles* (Vertigo/DC Comics, 1994), to mark gateway moments in the lives of the characters. Barbelith also operates in *The*

Invisibles as a sentient satellite stationed on the dark side of the moon that functions as a psychic placenta for humanity....

My *Neo-Scientific Novella* subtitle comes from Jarry's book, *Exploits and Opinions of Doctor Faustroll, Pataphysician*, which he called a *Neo-Scientific Novel*. Despite this description, Jarry's book defies any genre, and narrative elements such as plot, setting, and character development are constructed in the service of deeper explorations of language and 'pataphysics, his science of imaginary solutions, where improbable, imaginative hypotheses are more fruitful to investigations of reality than ordinary, verisimilar approaches.

In my novella, the character "Aletheia" is named for a Greek word that is usually translated into English as "truth" but which has been retranslated by Martin Heidegger in *Poetry, Language, Thought* (Harper Perennial, 2001 edition) as "unconcealedness." The character "Epoché" is named for a Greek term that means "the suspension of belief in the real world." The two join forces to stop a war. By using the words "Aletheia" and "Epoché" as the names of my characters, I want to propose that the state of being unconcealed, when combined in spacetime with the theoretical moment of suspending belief in the real world, can be a 'pataphysical response to war.

Blissymbols, an ideographic writing system invented by Charles K. Bliss (1897–1985) that consists of basic symbols, each representing a concept and joined to generate new symbols that represent new concepts, are reconceived in the story as a living language that was thought to be extinct.

One setting of the story is what Peter Lamborn Wilson/Hakim Bey calls the "temporary autonomous zones," where the poetic imagination is free to reign.

In addition to referencing my own two previous books in the novella, the first as an object (*iEpiphany*), the second as a setting (*Multiversal*), the three identifiable characters are joined by a nameless "she," an authorial "I," and unidentified language, the poetry—or what I melodramatically think of as U+F+O+L+A+N+G+U+A+G+E—all metafictional gestures that collide with the work's multiple forms in my attempt to amplify the hallucinatory encounters between points of view. By shape shifting among forms approximating fiction, poetry, and memoir, I am also striving to cross expectations of genre in order to make discoveries about what I see as any exploratory work's mutable carrier: inquiry itself.

NOTES

The chapter, "Variegated Passages," is based on the chapter, "Concerning the Dogfaced Baboon Bosse-de-Nage, Who Knew No Human Words but 'Ha Ha,'" after Plato, in various passages, from *Alfred Jarry's Exploits & Opinions of Doctor Faustroll, Pataphysician: A Neo-Scientific Novel*, trans. Simon Watson Taylor (Exact Change, 2001).

The chapter title, "How To Construct a Time Machine," is from an essay of the same name by Jarry in *Selected Works of Alfred Jarry* (Grove Press, 1980). The chapter titles, "The Becoming of Memory" and "The Imaginary Present," are phrases in Jarry's essay.

The chapter, "Let There Be Love," is after Alfred Jarry's novel, *Absolute Love* in *Three Early Novels, Collected Works II* (Atlas Press, 2006).

The chapter title, "The Origin of the Work of Art," and the name of the character, "Aletheia," are from Martin Heidegger's *Poetry, Language, Thought* (Harper Perennial, 2001 edition).

The name of the character, the "Enduring Karmanaut," is inspired by Peter Milligan and Brendan McCarthy's comic book, *Rogan Gosh: Star of the East* (DC Comics/Vertigo, 1994).

References to the "temporary autonomous zones" are indebted to Peter Lamborn Wilson/Hakim Bey's *The Temporary Autonomous Zone, Ontological Anarchy, Poetic Terrorism* (Autonomedia, anti-copyright 1985).

ACKNOWLEDGEMENTS

Thank you to the following writers and editors for publishing excerpts of this work in literary journals and other projects: Brian Lucas, *Poetbook*; John Gallaher, *The Laurel Review*; E. Tracy Grinnell, *Aufgabe*; Jerome Rothenberg, *Poems and Poetics*; Maxine Chernoff and Paul Hoover, *New American Writing*; Christian Peet and Guest Editor Bhanu Kapil, *Tarpaulin Sky Journal*; Nate Pritts and Guest Editor Darcie Dennigan, *H_NGM_N*; Junior Burke and Maureen Owen, *not enough night*; and Johannes Göransson and Joyelle McSweeney, *Action Yes*.

Thank you to my family and friends for their love and support, including Attilio and Cathy Catanzano, Patricia McCabe, Charles Catanzano, Rachel McCabe, and Holly McCabe; to Carmen Giménez Smith, Evan Lavender-Smith, Mike Meginnis, and J. Michael Martinez of Noemi Press for publishing this work, selecting it for the Noemi Press Book Award for Fiction, and giving me the opportunity to design the interior pages; to Andrew Joron and Bhanu Kapil for inspiration and their responses to this work; to Robert Bringhurst, poet, translator, and author of the seminal book, *The Elements of Typographical Style,* for his generosity in providing support on the interior design; to Paula Gillen, Susan Quasha, and Matt Baird for their friendship and support on the interior; to Laura Moriarty for inspiring this project with her novel, *Ultravioleta* (Atelos Press, 2006) and sparking my interest in Alfred Jarry's writing; to Shanxing Wang for his question about 4th person narration in his book, *Mad Science in Imperial City* (Futurepoem Books, 2005); to Amy

Pommerening for introducing me to the term, "epoché"; to Hugh Grant and Maya Wright of the Kirkland Museum of Decorative & Fine Art for the use of Vance Kirkland's painting, *Four Suns in Space*; to Alastair Brotchie and Chris Allen of Atlas Press in London for giving me books by Alfred Jarry and others; and to Sreedevi Bringi for her feedback on some of the scientific language in the chapter, "Shared Axiom."

Amy Catanzano is the author of two previous books. *Multiversal* (Fordham University Press, 2009) received the PEN USA Literary Award in Poetry and was selected for publication by Michael Palmer as the recipient of Fordham University's Poets Out Loud Prize. *iEpiphany* was published in 2008 by Anne Waldman's Erudite Fangs Editions. An e-chapbook of poems, *the heartbeat is a fractal*, was published in 2009 by Ahadada Books. Her essays on quantum poetics and the intersections of literature, science, and 'pataphysics have appeared in Jerome Rothenberg's *Poems and Poetics* and elsewhere. She is an Assistant Professor of English and the Director of the Creative Writing Program at Wake Forest University in Winston-Salem, North Carolina. She is also a regular guest faculty member in the Summer Writing Program of the Jack Kerouac School of Disembodied Poetics at Naropa University in Boulder, Colorado. She has an M.F.A. from the Iowa Writers' Workshop.